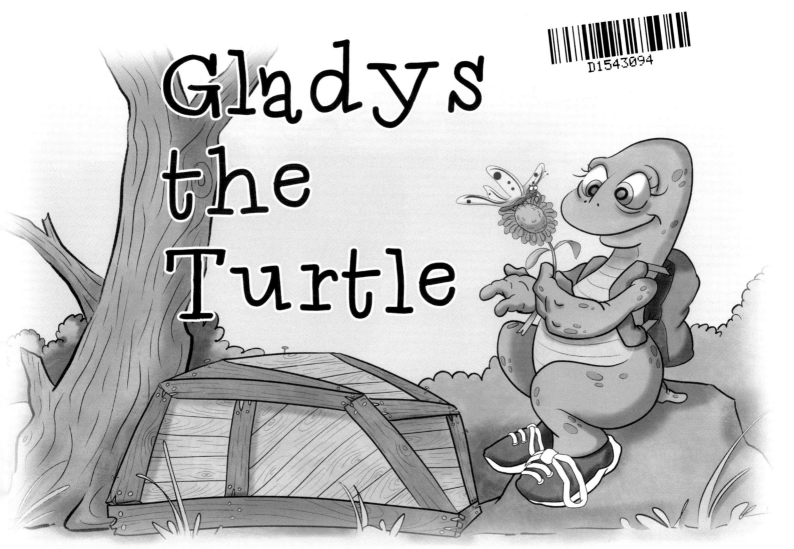

Gladys the Turtle

By: Jack Skeen

Illustrator: Chris Westra

Not her mom. Not her dad. Not her little brother. The whole idea of having a shell didn't make sense to her. "Who needs a shell?" she wondered. "Not me!"

Gladys was a turtle who didn't have a shell. In fact, she had never seen a turtle who had a shell.

1

She played in the stream, danced in the rain, chased butterflies, jumped rope and was very happy.

She never thought about what might happen if she said the wrong thing, or didn't do what someone wanted her to do.

She never worried about getting hurt.

4

One day, Gladys was taking a walk in her favorite red shoes, and she met some new kids who had just moved into the neighborhood.

They all had shells but it didn't matter to Gladys, she just wanted to be friends. 6

She showed them her red shoes. "How do you like my shoes?" she asked. "Aren't they beautiful?"

But they all laughed at her "Those are the ugliest shoes I have ever seen.", The biggest turtle said. 8

...went right to her room and slammed the door.

10

Her mother and father invited her to go to the park and to play in the stream but Gladys said she didn't feel like it.

She didn't want to get hurt again.

She only wanted to feel safe. But does this mean I have to stay in my room forever? she wondered.

12

Then she got an idea.
She decided she would build
a shell for herself,
and so she did.

She worked on it day and night...

...and finally it was ready.

14

The very next day she put it on and went outside. Her shell was heavy and hard to walk in. She couldn't dance in the rain or play in the steam.

She couldn't

jump rope either.

That didn't make her happy. But she did feel safe

15

No one could hardly even see her in this shell!

16

Wherever she went she peeked out of her shell to see if everything was okay. If she saw anything that seemed scary she shut her shell tight and waited until it was gone. She really didn't like having to live in her shell but her shell protected her kind heart.

Life was not so happy for Gladys.

Now she worried about being hurt all of the time. She told herself that being safe was the most important thing of all.

Gladys longed for somewhere she could live outside her shell again.

Then she got an idea!

19

She decided to start a club for turtles like herself who wanted to live outside their shells.

She wrote a list of rules each turtle
would have to accept:

1. Turtles will only
   be friends

2. Turtles will never
   be mean to
   each other.

3. Turtles will help each
   other whenever
   they can.

4 Turtles will never laugh at
   or tease each other.

5. Turtles will believe in

each other's dreams.

She posted her rules on the clubhouse door.
Soon other turtles started showing up.
They liked her rules.

They checked their shells at the front door.
Inside the clubhouse they played games...

...they danced in the rain, they jumped rope together and most of all they were happy and free.

"Who needs shells when one has friends?"
Gladys said happy at last.